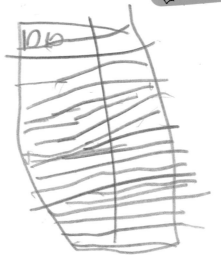

# Q is for

## AN ALPHABET

CLARION BOOKS

NEW YORK

# Duck

## GUESSING GAME

BY MARY ELTING
& MICHAEL FOLSOM

PICTURES BY JACK KENT

*P is for Jamie and S is for Raphael*

Clarion Books
a Houghton Mifflin Company imprint
215 Park Avenue South, New York, NY 10003
Text copyright © 1980 by Mary Elting and Michael Folsom
Pictures copyright © 1980 by Jack Kent

*Library of Congress Cataloging in Publication Data*

Elting, Mary, 1906-    Q is for duck.
Summary: While learning some facts about animals, the
reader is challenged to guess why A is for zoo, B is for dog,
and C is for hen.
[1. Alphabet. 2. Animals] I. Folsom, Michael, joint author.
II. Kent, Jack, 1920-    III. Title.
PZ7.E53Qab    [E]    80-13854
RNF ISBN 0-395-29437-1   PAP ISBN 0-395-30062-2

WOZ   20   19   18

# A is for Zoo

TICKETS

ZOO
ENTRANCE →

Why?

Because…

Animals live in the Zoo

# B is for Dog

Why?

Because a Dog **B**arks

# C is for Hen

Why?

Because a Hen Clucks

# D is for Mole

Why?

Because a Mole Digs

**E** is for Whale

Why?

Because...

a Whale is $\mathrm{E}$normous

# F is for Bird

Why?

Because a Bird Flies

# G is for Horse

Why?

Because a Horse Gallops

# H  is for Owl

Why?

Because an Owl **H**oots

# I is for Mosquito

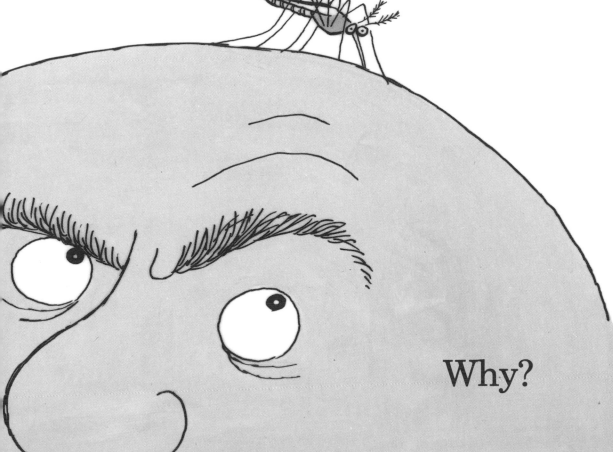

Why?

Because
Mosquito bites Itch

# J

is for Kangaroo

Why?

Because a Kangaroo Jumps

# K is for Mule

Why?

Because a Mule Kicks

# L is for Frog

Why?

Because a Frog Leaps

**M** is for Cow

Why?

Because a Cow **M**oos

# N is for Cat

Why?

Because a Cat Naps

O is for Pig

Why?

Because a Pig **O**inks

# P is for Chick

Why?

Because a Chick Peeps

# Q is for Duck

Why?

Because a Duck **Q**uacks

# R

is for Lion

Why?

# ROAR

Because a Lion Roars

# S is for Camel

Why?

Because a Camel Spits

# T is for Elephant

Why?

Because
an Elephant Trumpets

# U is for Prairie Dog

Why?

Because Prairie Dogs live

# Underground

V is for Chameleon

Why?

Because a
Chameleon seems to Vanish

# W is for Snake

Why?

Because a Snake Wiggles

 is for Dinosaur

Why?

Because Dinosaurs are

e**X**tinct

# Y is for Coyote

Why?

Because a Coyote **Y**owls

Z is for Animals

Why?

Because
Animals live in the Zoo